SHE ARRIVED

For the young woman who is figuring it out

Kendra Tamika

Remember Her Publishing

She Arrived

Published by Remember Her Publishing

ISBN: 979-8-9954705-8-8

LCCN: 2026910981

First Edition

Printed in the United States of America

She Arrived is part of the Remember Her Girls Series published by Remember Her Publishing. The Nova character, while inspired by real experiences, is a fictional composite. Any resemblance to specific persons living or dead is coincidental.

She Arrived is written for young women ages 18 to 25 navigating the transition to adulthood. It contains mature themes including relationships, financial independence, and identity that are appropriate for this age group.

For the young woman who is figuring it out.

You are not behind.
You are not lost.
You are not failing.

You are in the middle of becoming.
And becoming takes exactly as long as it takes.

Give yourself the grace
you would give your best friend.
All of it.
Without conditions.
Starting now.

She arrived.
And so will you.

TABLE OF CONTENTS

A NOTE FROM THE AUTHOR

Nova remembered herself at twelve.

She rose at fifteen.

She arrived at eighteen.

Not at a destination. Not at a finish line. Not at a place where everything was figured out and the uncertainty was behind her and the path forward was clear and well-lit and free of obstacles.

She arrived at herself.

Which was always the only place worth going.

This book is for the young woman who is in the middle of that journey. Who is eighteen or nineteen or twenty-two and standing at the beginning of something enormous and feeling, sometimes, like everyone else around her knows something she does not. Like she is the only one who is still figuring it out.

You are not the only one.

Everyone is figuring it out.

The ones who look the most certain are often the ones working the hardest to appear that way.

This book is what I wish someone had handed me at eighteen. Before the years of learning things the hard way that I could have learned with more grace if someone had simply said them out loud.

I am saying them out loud now.

For you.

With love,

Kendra Tamika

CHAPTER 1

The Gap Year Nobody Told You To Take

Everyone has an opinion about what I should do next.
College applications.
Scholarship deadlines.
Five year plans.
Everyone wants to know the plan.
I have a plan.
It just does not look like what they expected.
It looks like this:
One year.
Just me.
The work.
The becoming.
Before anything else.
Before anyone else.
That is the plan.
I am at peace with it.
Mostly.
Ask me again in six months.

The morning Nova told her parents she was taking a gap year her father made pancakes.

Not because pancakes were a response to significant news in the Cole household. Because it was Saturday and Saturday mornings had always meant pancakes: the specific ritual of it, her father at the stove with the particular focused attention he brought to breakfast foods that he brought to very little else, the kitchen filling with the smell of butter and batter and the comfortable warmth of a morning that had nowhere urgent to be.

Nova sat at the kitchen table with her sketchbook open and her coffee and waited for the right moment.

There was no right moment.

She had been waiting for the right moment for three weeks.

"I am not applying to college this fall," she said.

Her father's spatula paused over the pan.

Her mother looked up from her phone.

The kitchen did not collapse. The world did not end.

"Tell me more," Reina said.

That was the thing about her mother that Nova had always relied on. Not the immediate reassurance. Not the reflexive concern. The invitation to say more. The specific quality of Reina's attention that made the space between I said a thing and what happens next feel safe enough to say the whole thing.

So Nova said the whole thing.

She had been thinking about it since June.

Since the National Showcase letter and the conversation with Mr. Osei and the first page of the new sketchbook that said sophomore year, Nova Cole, artist, National Showcase, she rose, and she is just beginning. She had written that and meant it completely and then spent the summer sitting with what just beginning actually required of her.

The college path was clear and available and real. Westbrook had generated genuine attention from art programs across the country. Her portfolio was strong. Applications were possible. The next step was right there waiting to be taken.

She had looked at it for the entire summer.

And she had felt, not reluctance exactly, not fear, but a specific quality of not-readiness that she had learned over years of honest self-assessment to take seriously. The feeling was not I cannot do this. It was I am not finished with what I am doing here yet.

She was in the middle of something.

The gap year was not an avoidance of the next chapter.

It was the completion of the current one.

"What does the year look like?" her father asked.

"I want to develop the new series," she said. "The one I started at the end of sophomore year. It needs more than I can give it while I'm also managing a full academic schedule." She paused. "I want to build the business side. The prints. The commissions. The platform. I want to understand what it means to be a working artist before I go to school to study being a working artist."

"And?" Reina said. Because there was an and and her mother always heard the and.

"And I want to travel. Not expensively. Not far necessarily. But I want to see things I haven't seen. I want to go to museums I've never been to. I want to be in rooms with work that exists outside my specific experience and let it affect me before I know what I think about it."

She looked at her parents.

"I want one year of being fully myself before I step into the next structure," she said. "I think I need it. I think the work needs it. I think the woman I am trying to become needs it."

Reina and her father looked at each other across the table. The specific look of two people who had been parenting the same person for eighteen years and had developed a private language of glances that communicated entire conversations in a second.

"You have thought about this," her father said.

"Since June," Nova confirmed.

"You have a plan."

"I have a plan."

"Show us the plan," Reina said.

Nova opened her sketchbook to the pages she had prepared. Not a formal presentation. But the specific organization of someone who had done the work of thinking something through completely before bringing it to the people whose response mattered.

She had mapped the year. The financial projection. The studio time allocation. The travel plans. The portfolio development goals. The business infrastructure she intended to build.

Her parents looked at the pages.

"The financial projection is conservative," Reina said finally.

"Intentionally," Nova said. "I would rather plan for less and deliver more than the other way around."

Reina looked at her daughter.

"You sound like me," she said.

"I know," Nova said.

Here is what I want to tell you about the gap year nobody told you to take.

It is not a gap.

That word implies absence: a space where something should be but is not. A missing piece. A delay in the real thing. The gap year is described by the world as the thing you do instead of the next thing, which immediately positions it as lesser. As a deviation from the correct path.

It is not a gap.

It is a foundation.

The specific year, or months, or season, or however long you give yourself, of intentional becoming before you step into the next structure. The year of learning who you are when nobody is grading you. When nobody is measuring your progress against a rubric that someone else designed. When the only standard is the one you set and the only accountability is the one you hold yourself to.

That year is not nothing.

That year is everything.

Nova spent the first month of her gap year doing what she had always done when the world gave her unstructured time.

She drew.

Not toward anything. Not in preparation for anything. Just drawing, the way she had drawn since she was nine years old in her pink room before she understood what the practice was building in her.

She drew for three to four hours every morning.

At the end of the first month she looked at what she had made.

Thirty full pages. Three times her usual monthly output. The work was different from anything she had produced during the structured school years. Not better technically. Different in a quality that was harder to name.

Freer.

Like the work that came from a hand that was not carrying anything other than the work itself.

She wrote in her sketchbook:

> *The gap year nobody told me to take is the most productive thing I have ever done.*
>
> *Not because of what I made.*
>
> *Because of what I learned about how I make.*
>
> *About who I am when I am not performing for any audience.*
>
> *About what comes out of me when I stop managing the output.*

This is the foundation.
Everything else I build, the college, the career, the life,
will be built on top of this.
And it will hold.
Because I built it myself.
From the truth.
That is the only foundation that holds.

Your frontal lobe is not fully developed until you are twenty-five.

I am not telling you this to make you feel like your decisions do not count or your feelings are not real or your sense of who you are is just a preliminary draft that does not matter yet. Your decisions count. Your feelings are real. Your sense of who you are is as true as it has ever been and truer than it was last year.

I am telling you this because I want you to extend yourself the specific grace of being in process.

The part of your brain responsible for long-term consequence assessment, for fully integrating who you are with how you behave, for the kind of wisdom that comes from having made enough mistakes to know what they teach you, that part is still being built. Right now. While you are reading this.

That is not a flaw.

That is the design.

You are supposed to be in process at this age. The world has been lying to you when it tells you that you should have it figured out. That you should know what you want to do for the rest of your life at eighteen.

You have time.

Give yourself the gap.

Not from your life.

Into it.

Nova took three trips during her gap year.

The first was to a city three hours north where a museum she had been wanting to visit for two years was running a retrospective of a graphic novelist whose work had influenced her development more than almost anything else she had encountered. She went alone. Took the train. Stayed in an inexpensive hotel for two nights. Spent nine hours across two days in that museum.

She filled forty pages of her sketchbook in response.

Not copies of the work. Responses. The specific visual conversation between her hand and someone else's vision that happened when you gave art the time it deserved.

The second trip was a day trip to a gallery in the arts district of a city nearby that was showing the work of three emerging illustrators, artists within ten years of her own age, artists whose careers were in the early stages she was about to enter. She went and looked and paid honest attention.

She went home and raised her print prices.

Not out of arrogance. Out of the honest assessment of someone who had looked at the market and understood her position within it.

The third trip was with Reina.

They went to galleries. They ate well. They talked, the real kind, the kind that only happened when you were in unfamiliar geography and the ordinary landmarks of your shared life were not present to organize the conversation around familiar patterns.

They had the lunch.

The one Nova had been building toward for months without knowing it.

"Who were you before you were my mom?" she asked.

Reina put down her fork.

She was quiet for a moment.

And then she told her.

She Arrived — Reflection

- ◆ What is the thing you are in the middle of right now that deserves to be finished before you rush into the next structure?
- ◆ What does your version of the gap year look like, not literally, but in spirit? What would one year of intentional becoming actually require of you?
- ◆ What would you make, what would come out of you, if you gave yourself one month of working without any audience, without any grade, without any external measurement of whether it was good?
- ◆ Where in your life are you performing productivity rather than actually building something real?

> *I am not behind. I am not lost. I am in the middle of something real and I am going to give it the time it deserves. My becoming is not a gap. It is a foundation. And I am building it well.*

She Arrived

Give yourself the gap. Not from your life. Into it. The foundation you build in this season will hold everything that comes after. Take the time. Do the work. Become who you are before the world tells you who to be.

CHAPTER 2

Leave Home Before You Leave Home

We are in a city neither of us has been to before.
No history here.
No associations.
Just new streets and new restaurants
and my mother sitting across from me
looking like herself.
Not my mother.
Herself.
I have been looking at her my whole life.
I think I am only now starting to see her.

The restaurant they chose together was small and warm and had the particular quality of places that had been doing the same thing well for a long time without needing to announce it. Exposed brick. Candles on the tables. A menu that was short enough to mean everything on it was worth ordering.

They had walked past it on the way back from the second gallery of the day and both stopped at exactly the same moment, neither one having said anything, both of them simply stopping and turning toward the door with the synchronized instinct of two people who had been sharing space long enough to have developed the same reflexes.

"This one," Reina had said.

"Yeah," Nova had agreed.

They were shown to a table by the window. Nova ordered the pasta. Reina ordered the fish. They split the bread that came first and did not talk about anything important for the first twenty minutes: the galleries they had seen, the piece in the second one that they had both stood in front of for longer than either of them had planned, the quality of the city they were in.

The comfortable conversation of two people who knew each other well enough to not need to perform engagement.

And then the bread was gone and the pasta had arrived and Nova put down her fork and asked the question she had been building toward for months without knowing that was what she was doing.

"Who were you before you were my mom?"

Reina set down her own fork.

The question landed in the space between them, not heavily, not with the weight of confrontation, but with the weight of something real being asked by someone who genuinely wanted to know.

She was quiet for a moment. Not the quiet of someone deciding whether to answer. The quiet of someone deciding where to start.

"How far back do you want me to go?" she said.

"All the way," Nova said.

Reina looked at her daughter across the table. At the eighteen year old woman with her father's eyes and her grandmother's locs and her own particular way of sitting in a chair, slightly forward, attentive, sketchbook on the table beside her plate because the sketchbook was always on the table.

"I was a girl who liked music first," Reina said. "Before anything else. Before motherhood and marriage and all of the things I became, I was a girl who played piano and sang in the church choir and believed for a long time that music was going to be the thing." She paused. "I was good at it. Not exceptional. But good. Good enough that people noticed. Good enough that for a few years it felt like a real possibility."

"What happened to it?" Nova asked.

"Life happened," Reina said simply. "The way it does. The music became a smaller part of the picture as other things became larger. I stopped playing seriously sometime in my early twenties and I have always carried a small grief about that." She said it without drama. As a fact. "Not a devastating grief. Just the specific sadness of something you put down and never quite picked back up."

Nova thought about the sketchbook in the bag in sixth grade.

She thought about January.

She thought about carrying it in her hand.

"Do you wish someone had told you not to put it down?" she asked.

Reina looked at her.

"I wish someone had told me it was allowed to coexist with everything else," she said. "That choosing the other things, the family, the work, the life I was building, did not have to mean abandoning the music. That I could have had both." She paused. "That is the lie I believed. That adulthood required you to choose. That the serious things and the beautiful things lived in separate rooms and you had to decide which room to live in."

"They don't," Nova said. "Live in separate rooms."

"No," Reina agreed. "But I did not know that then." She picked up her fork. "You know it. That is different. That is better."

They talked for three hours.

The pasta went cold. Reina ordered tea. Nova ordered more water and forgot to drink it. The restaurant filled and emptied around them and they did not notice because they were in the specific absorbed quality of a conversation that had been waiting to happen for a long time and had finally found its moment.

Reina told her about the years before Nova. About the relationships that had taught her things she had not wanted to learn at the time. About the business, the first version of it, the version that had been taken and the version she had built back from nothing with her own hands and her own recipe and the fierce quiet determination of a woman who understood that the thing she had created was hers regardless of what anyone else tried to claim.

She told her about the hospital.

Not all of it. There were parts of that story that were still being processed. But enough. The room with the grayish green walls. The morning she had been wheeled into emergency surgery and the person who should have been there had been somewhere else.

The first time she had said yes when she meant no.

"I want you to know that story," Reina said. "Not so you feel sorry for me. I am past the need for that." She looked at her daughter directly. "So that when the moment comes for you, and it will come, it comes for everyone, you will recognize it. The moment when someone is asking you to make yourself smaller to make them more comfortable. The moment when you are about to say yes and you mean no." She paused. "I want you to recognize it faster than I did."

Nova sat with that.

"How will I recognize it?" she asked.

"Your body will tell you," Reina said. "The same way it always tells you. The same way it told you in sixth grade when Kayla said that word in the hallway and something in you went cold." She reached across the table and touched her daughter's hand briefly. "You have always known. The work of your life is learning to trust what you know."

Here is what leaving home before you leave home actually means.

It means examining the instructions you were given before you carry them into the rest of your life.

Not to dismantle them. Not to perform a dramatic rejection of where you came from. But to look at them honestly and decide consciously what you are keeping and what you are releasing.

Because you absorbed things.

We all absorbed things.

The way adults around you navigated conflict. The way they talked about money. The way they moved through romantic relationships, what they accepted, what they tolerated, what they left and what they stayed for. The way they talked about their own worth.

You absorbed all of it.

Before you had the language to evaluate it.

Before you had the experience to know whether it was true.

And now you are at the age where you have both, the language and some of the experience, and you can look at what you absorbed and ask the question that nobody in your childhood was in a position to ask for you.

Is this mine? Did I choose this? Does this serve the woman I am becoming?

Have the conversation.

Before you leave for college. Before you move across the country. Before the geography changes and the distance makes the conversation harder to have.

Have it now.

Sit across from your mother, or your grandmother or your auntie or the woman who has loved you longest, and ask her who she was before she was yours.

Not to take something from her. To give her something. The specific gift of being seen as a full person by the person whose opinion of her matters most.

And receive what she gives back.

Because she is going to give you the map.

Not a map to her life. But the map to yourself. The understanding of where your patterns came from. The inheritance, both the beautiful parts worth carrying and the heavy parts worth setting down.

She was figuring it out.

She was always figuring it out.

The same as you.

That knowledge is one of the most liberating things you will ever receive.

Ask for it.

Who were you before you were mine?

Ask it.

And listen to all of it.

She Arrived — Reflection

◆ What do you know about the woman who raised you before she was yours? What do you not know that you could ask?

◆ What patterns do you see in your own life that might have started in hers? Which ones are worth keeping? Which ones are yours to change?

◆ What would it mean to take her hand, not as a child reaching for safety but as a woman walking beside another woman as an equal?

◆ What is something you absorbed from watching the adults around you that you have never consciously examined?

> *I examine what I have inherited. I keep what serves me. I release what does not. Not as a rejection of where I came from. As a continuation of it. The next generation always goes further. I am the next generation. I go further. With love and with intention. Starting now.*

She Arrived

She was figuring it out the whole time. Just like you. Just like every woman before you. The map was always available. You just had to ask for it.

CHAPTER 3

Learn Yourself Before You Love Someone Else

Someone asked me today if I was seeing anyone.
I said no.
They said: why not?
Like no was a problem to be solved.
Like being eighteen and single
was a condition requiring explanation.
I thought about how to answer.
I said: I am seeing myself.
They laughed like I was joking.
I was not joking.

Nova had a theory about the way the world talked to young women about love.

The theory was this: that the world began asking young women about their romantic lives approximately three years before it began asking them about their professional lives, and that this sequence was not accidental. That the consistent cultural message, who are you with arriving long before what are you building, had a specific effect on the internal architecture of a young woman's priorities. That it trained the attention outward before it had finished developing inward.

She had been thinking about this theory since she was fifteen.

She had been watching it operate on every girl she knew since she was twelve.

She had not been immune to it.

Marcus had happened. The warmth of being seen and the specific hurt of watching that warmth redirect. She had moved through it. She was proud of that. She had the sketchbook entry to prove it.

I did not shrink. Not once. That is the whole lesson.

But she had also been honest with herself about how much of her sophomore year she had spent thinking about Marcus in the margins of thinking about her art.

She had let it matter too much.

Not catastrophically. Not in a way that had derailed her. But more than it should have.

She had let someone else's attention become a metric for her own worth.

She was not going to do that again.

Not yet. Not until she understood herself well enough to enter a relationship from a different place.

Not from wanting to be seen.

From already knowing she was worth seeing.

Here is what I want to tell you about love at eighteen.

Not that it is not real. It is.

Not that it is not important. It is.

But this, the specific thing that nobody said to me at eighteen and that I am saying to you now as directly as I know how:

Learn yourself before you love someone else.

Not because love will ruin you. It will not.

Because you deserve to know who you are before someone else starts having opinions about it.

Because the person you are at eighteen is still being formed. Still becoming. Still arriving at its final shape.

And the person you love at this stage will influence that shape.

Not necessarily for the worse. But significantly. In ways that will take years to fully understand.

The question is not whether to love.

The question is whether you are solid enough in your own foundation to love without losing yourself in the loving.

Nova spent a significant portion of her gap year alone.

Not lonely. Alone. There is a difference and she had understood the difference since she was eleven years old.

She was someone who needed solitude. Not as a retreat from the world but as a regular maintenance of herself, the specific practice of returning to her own interior, her own thoughts, her own pace, her own company. Without it she began to drift.

She protected her alone time during the gap year with the same intentionality she brought to her studio time.

She had breakfast alone most mornings. Happily. Deliberately. With a book or her sketchbook.

She took solo walks in the evenings. The specific neighborhood walking she had always loved.

She went to movies alone. This one had required the most internal negotiation. The cultural script around solo movie attendance was particularly loud. She had gone anyway.

She had loved it. Every single time.

The specific freedom of having an unmediated experience. Of responding to what was in front of her without the slight self-consciousness of being observed having the response.

She wrote in her sketchbook after the third solo movie: I am excellent company. I have been underutilizing myself.

She also dated.

This is the part that gets left out of the learn-yourself narrative, the implication that learning yourself requires complete romantic abstinence.

You do not have to choose.

Nova went on dates during the gap year. Not many. But some. Enough to understand what she was learning and to test the knowledge against real experience.

She went on two dates with a photographer she had met through a mutual connection. He was interesting and attractive and had good taste in films.

On the third date he said something, casually, not meanly, in the flow of a conversation about their respective work, that suggested he found her neurodivergence endearing in a way that made her feel like a novelty rather than a person.

She did not go on a fourth date.

Not in anger. With the clean clear certainty of someone who knew the difference between being seen and being collected. Between someone who was interested in who she was and someone who was interested in the idea of who she was.

She went home and wrote it down.

Non-negotiable. Real. From the beginning.
Not endearing.
Not a quirk.
Not a novelty.
Me.
If someone cannot understand the difference
they do not get access to the interior.
Full stop.

Here is what learning yourself before you love someone else actually produces.

Standards.

Not the checklist kind. Not a list of physical preferences and income requirements. That kind of list is an anxiety management tool dressed up as discernment.

The real standards.

The ones that come from knowing yourself well enough to know what you need. Not what you want. What you need. The things that are non-negotiable not because you decided they should be but because you discovered through honest self-examination that they are fundamental to your ability to be yourself in a relationship.

For Nova the non-negotiables were few and absolute.

Someone who made her more herself rather than less. This was the whole standard, really. She had learned in sixth grade what less herself felt like. She had carried that knowledge through high school and into her gap year and she was not going to unlearn it for anyone.

Someone who asked the real questions. Not the social questions. The questions that proved they were paying attention.

Someone who did not need her to be smaller to feel larger.

Three things. That was the whole list. Everything else was negotiable.

She called Simone on a Sunday evening in November.

"I figured out my non-negotiables," Nova said.

"Tell me," Simone said.

Nova told her. The three things. The photographer and the fourth date that did not happen.

Simone was quiet for a moment.

"I wish I had known mine at eighteen," she said.

"You were eighteen four months ago," Nova pointed out.

"I know. I wish I had known them at seventeen."

Nova smiled at her bedroom ceiling.

"What are yours?" she asked.

"Someone who laughs at the same things," Simone said without hesitation. "Not the same jokes. The same quality of funny. The absurdity. The thing that is funny because it is true rather than because it is performed."

"That's a really good one."

"I've been thinking about it since you called." A pause. "What made you figure yours out?"

Nova thought about it.

"The gap year," she said. "Having time to be with myself without the noise of everything else. I think I needed to know who I was alone before I could know what I needed from someone else."

"That's really mature," Simone said.

"I know," Nova said.

"You're not supposed to just say I know when someone says that."

"Why not? It's true. I am proud of me too." Nova paused. "I'm allowed to be."

Simone laughed. The real one. The one that had been starting in her chest since sixth grade.

"Yes," she said. "You absolutely are."

You are allowed to be proud of yourself.

I want to say that clearly because the instruction to be humble, which is valuable and worth keeping, sometimes gets confused with the instruction to be self-deprecating, which is not the same thing and is not worth keeping.

Humility means knowing your actual size. Not smaller than you are. Your actual size.

You are allowed to know your actual size.

You are allowed to look at what you have built and what you have survived and who you are becoming and feel the specific pride of someone who has been paying attention and doing the work.

That pride is not arrogance.

It is accurate.

And it is the foundation of everything.

Including love.

Especially love.

The pride you feel in yourself, the genuine evidence-based recognition of your own worth, is the thing that determines the quality of love you allow into your life.

Know your actual size.

Love from that place.

Not from wanting to be completed.

From wanting to share your completeness.

That is the difference.

That is everything.

She Arrived — Reflection

◆ What are your actual non-negotiables, not the checklist, not the preferences, but the core things you know you need in a relationship to remain fully yourself?

◆ When was the last time you were genuinely alone, not lonely, not scrolling, not filling the silence, just with yourself? What did you find there?

◆ What does loving from completeness rather than from wanting to be completed actually look like in your life?

◆ Have you ever let someone else's attention become a metric for your own worth? What did that cost you?

> *I am excellent company. I know my actual size. I am not looking for someone to complete me. I am already complete. I am looking for someone worthy of my completeness. And I will know them because in their presence I am more myself. Not less. Always more.*

She Arrived

Learn yourself before you love someone else. Not because love is dangerous but because you deserve to arrive at love knowing who you are. That way when someone tries to change you, you will notice. And you will know what to do.

CHAPTER 4

Your Money Is Your Freedom

I made my first four figures from my art today.
One thousand and forty-three dollars.
From prints and one commission.
I have been building toward this for six months.
I sat with the number for a long time.
Not because of what it bought.
Because of what it meant.
It meant: you can provide for yourself.
It meant: your gift is a viable thing.
It meant: the life you desire is buildable.
One thousand and forty-three dollars.
I have never felt wealthier in my life.

The first print Nova sold during her gap year went for thirty-five dollars.

She had priced it conservatively, had looked at comparable work from artists at her level and priced slightly below the midpoint, the cautious instinct of someone who was not yet certain the market would agree with her assessment of her own work's value.

It sold within four hours of being posted.

She looked at the notification. Thirty-five dollars.

She looked at it for a moment.

Then she raised the price of every remaining print by twenty dollars.

Not out of greed. Out of the honest recalibration of someone who had just received useful market information and was adjusting accordingly. The four-hour sell-through meant the original price had been too low. Not slightly too low. Significantly too low.

The revised prints sold too.

Not as quickly. But they sold.

And each sale arrived with the specific feeling she had been building toward all fall: the feeling of her work existing in the world as a thing of value. Not in the artistic sense, which she had understood for years. In the practical sense. In the sense that mattered for building a life.

Her work was worth money.

Her gift was a viable thing.

The life she desired was buildable.

Here is the thing about financial independence that nobody tells you when you are eighteen.

It is not about the amount.

It is about the message.

Every dollar you earn, every single dollar, regardless of whether it is thirty-five or thirty-five thousand, sends a message to yourself about what is possible. About what you are capable of generating. About the relationship between your gifts and the world's willingness to compensate you for them.

That message compounds.

Not the money. The message. The belief. The evidence you accumulate over time that you can do this.

This is why you start now.

Not because you will get rich at eighteen. You will not. But the message it sends, the specific confidence it builds in you about your own ability to provide for yourself through your work, that is the foundation.

The foundation of everything else.

Nova read The Richest Man in Babylon during the gap year.

Her mother had mentioned it once, years ago, casually, in the context of a conversation about money. Nova had remembered the title. Had looked it up during the gap year when she was thinking seriously about the financial architecture of her life.

She read it in two days.

A portion of everything you earn belongs to you first.

Not the portion that is left after everything else. A portion set aside first, before any expense is paid. Ten percent was the ancient recommendation. Nova decided on fifteen.

From every print sale, every commission, every dollar that came in during the gap year, fifteen percent went directly into an account she did not touch.

Not for anything. Not for an emergency. Not for an opportunity. For her future self.

Fifteen percent. Always. First.

She also kept a record.

Every dollar in. Every dollar out. Not in a formal accounting system. In her sketchbook. A simple two-column list. Incoming. Outgoing. Reviewed every Sunday morning over coffee before the week began.

Five minutes. That was all it took.

And what she discovered in those five Sunday mornings was something that should not have been surprising but was: she was spending money in ways she had not been fully aware of. The accumulated small purchases that happened in the absence of attention.

She made two adjustments.

She stopped buying things that were available to her more cheaply somewhere else because the convenience of the expensive version felt like a small luxury she deserved.

She started buying better materials for her work. The high-quality paper. The specific pencils that lasted longer.

The first adjustment saved her money.

The second investment made her money: the quality of the work produced on better materials was measurably different and the prints sold at a higher price point.

Better inputs. Better outputs.

That applied to everything.

Nova had a conversation with her father about money during the gap year that she had not expected to be as significant as it turned out to be.

He was not a wealthy man. He had not built the kind of financial legacy that came with dramatic stories.

What he had was something less dramatic and more durable.

He had never spent more than he earned.

For his entire adult life. Through lean years and more comfortable years.

"That sounds simple," Nova said.

"It is simple," he said. "It is also the hardest thing most people never manage to do."

"Why don't they do it?"

He thought about it.

"Because the distance between what you earn and what you can spend on credit is the distance between who you are and who you want to appear to be," he said. "And most people would rather appear to be further along than they are than live honestly within the life they have actually built."

Nova wrote that down immediately.

The distance between what you earn and what you can spend on credit is the distance between who you are and who you want to appear to be.

She thought about it every time she made a financial decision for the rest of the gap year.

Here is what I want you to understand about money at eighteen.

It is not a separate category of your life.

It is woven into everything. Into your freedom. Into your choices. Into the quality of love you allow yourself. Into whether you stay in situations that do not serve you because leaving them feels financially impossible.

A woman without financial independence is a woman whose choices are constrained by other people's resources.

A woman with financial independence is a woman who chooses freely.

You want to be the second woman.

You start building her now.

Not by earning a lot. By managing what you have with intention. By putting yourself first in the allocation. By knowing where every dollar goes.

By never spending more than you earn.

By investing something, anything, even something small, in things that grow without your constant attention.

By understanding that the lifestyle you desire is buildable. Not all at once. Not without effort. But buildable. Systematically. With the specific patience of someone who has decided that the long game is worth playing.

Ask yourself the question that changed everything for Nova.

What is the lifestyle I desire?

Not what you can currently afford. Not what seems realistic. Not what other people your age seem to be living.

The lifestyle you desire. Specific. Detailed. Felt.

Write it down. In present tense. As if it is already happening.

And then, practically, without drama, in the patient way of someone who has decided to build rather than wish, figure out what the baseline number is. The minimum monthly income that gets you to the foundation of that life.

That number is your target. Not your ceiling. Your floor.

Start now. With what you have. It is enough to start.

She Arrived — Reflection

- ◆ What is the lifestyle you desire, specifically, in detail, felt? Have you ever allowed yourself to want it out loud?
- ◆ What is the floor, the minimum monthly income that gets you to the baseline of that life? Do you know your number?
- ◆ What is one financial habit you could start today, no matter how small, that your future self would thank you for?
- ◆ Are you living at the level of who you are or at the level of who you want to appear to be?

> *My financial freedom is an act of self love. I put myself first in the allocation. I know where my money goes. I build toward the life I desire. Every intentional dollar is a brick in the foundation of my freedom. I am building. Every day. Starting now.*

She Arrived

A woman with financial independence is a woman who chooses freely. Build that woman. Starting with fifteen percent. Starting with the Sunday check-in. Starting with knowing your number. Start now. With what you have.

CHAPTER 5

The Circle That Deserves You

Simone called me at midnight last night.
Not because anything was wrong.
Just because she had been thinking about something
and wanted to tell me before she went to sleep.
We talked for two hours.
That is what the right circle feels like.
Not the people who show up when it is convenient.
The people who call at midnight
because the thought could not wait
and they knew you would answer.
I answered.
I always answer.
That is what we built.
That is what the right circle is.

Nova had been thinking about circles since October.

Not abstractly. Specifically. With the particular focused attention she brought to things she wanted to understand completely. She had been observing the people in her life with the honest clarity of someone who had the time and the distance to see clearly.

What she saw was this.

She had approximately thirty people she would call acquaintances. People she liked. People she was glad existed in her life in the specific ambient way that acquaintances existed. She wished them well. She did not share her interior with them.

She had approximately eight people she would call friends. People she had built something with over time. Genuine fondness. The specific warmth of knowing and being known at a level that went beyond the surface.

And she had the inner circle.

Four people.

Simone. Jordan. Her parents.

Four people who had full access.

To the unedited version. To the uncertain work before it was posted. To the real answer when they asked how she was doing. To the interior, the actual interior, not the curated version she presented to the world.

Four people.

That was it.

That was enough.

She had released two people during the gap year.

Not dramatically. Not with confrontation or declaration. With the quiet deliberate fade of someone who had understood that certain relationships were not serving the woman she was becoming and had simply, gradually, kindly, without cruelty, stopped investing in them.

The first was a girl from high school she had maintained a friendship with out of history rather than genuine connection. They had known each other since freshman year. Had texted regularly. Had met for lunch occasionally. Had performed the ongoing friendship with all the expected gestures.

But the actual conversations had been performances. Two people doing friendship rather than having it.

She stopped initiating.

The other girl stopped initiating too.

Within three months the friendship had ended without either of them having to say so.

Nova had expected to feel guilty about this.

She felt something else entirely.

Relief.

The specific relief of releasing energy that had been quietly draining without her fully noticing it. Like setting down a bag she had been carrying for so long she had stopped registering the weight.

The second release was harder.

A boy from the arts community she had been circling around for months. Not romantically, or not only romantically. He was funny and talented and had the specific kind of charisma that made people want to be near him and he had been directing that charisma at Nova with enough consistency that she had begun to wonder if there was something there.

And then she had paid attention to how she felt after their interactions.

Every time.

Not during. During was fine. The conversations were good. The energy was high.

After.

After she felt slightly less than she had felt before. Not dramatically. Just slightly smaller. Slightly more self-conscious.

She recognized the feeling.

She had felt a version of it in sixth grade every time she put the sketchbook in the bag.

She stopped circling.

Here is what I know about the inner circle after eighteen years of building and rebuilding and examining mine.

The right people do not require you to earn their attention.

They give it freely. Not carelessly. Carefully. But freely. Without the exhausting calculus of wondering whether you are being interesting enough or impressive enough to deserve continued inclusion.

The right people celebrate your wins without a shadow in it.

This is the one I had to learn to recognize. The shadow, the slight dimming, the almost-invisible hesitation before the congratulations, the compliment that somehow lands as a comparison rather than a celebration. You will feel it before you can name it. Trust the feeling. The right people are simply, genuinely happy for you. Without the shadow.

The right people tell you the truth.

Not harshly. Not as a weapon. With the specific kindness of someone who loves you enough to be honest because they know the truth serves you better than comfortable agreement.

Simone had been doing this since sixth grade.

Nova had a conversation with Jordan during the gap year that reoriented something.

Jordan was at university now, an art program in the northeast, exactly where her work had been pointing since freshman year at Westbrook.

Jordan called on a Tuesday.

"I am thinking about changing my focus," she said without preamble. "From sequential art to installation. There is a professor here who is doing work that is changing the way I think about what I want to make."

Nova was quiet for a moment.

"Tell me about the work," she said.

Jordan told her. Fifteen minutes of description: the specific installation pieces, the conceptual framework, the way it related to everything Jordan had already been doing and expanded it into a larger space.

Nova listened.

"What is stopping you?" she asked when Jordan finished.

"I have been the sequential art person for four years," Jordan said. "My whole identity here is built on that work. Changing feels like abandoning something."

"Is the new work honest?" Nova asked.

"Yes."

"More honest than the sequential work?"

A pause.

"Different honest," Jordan said finally. "Like a different frequency of the same truth."

"Then it is not abandoning anything," Nova said. "It is expanding. The sequential art made you the person who can do the installation work. You are not leaving it. You are going further with it."

Jordan was quiet.

"You sound like Mr. Osei," she said.

"He is in all of our heads," Nova said. "Permanently. We should send him a thank you card."

Jordan laughed. "We really should."

"Change your focus," Nova said. "Make the honest work. That is the whole instruction."

Jordan changed her focus.

Six months later she was selected for a prestigious installation fellowship.

That was what the right circle did.

Not just celebrated you.

Called you forward.

Here is how to know who belongs in your inner circle.

Ask yourself one question about each person.

Do I feel more like myself or less like myself after spending time with them?

That is the whole test.

Not: do I enjoy their company? You can enjoy someone's company and still feel slightly less yourself afterward.

Not: do they mean well? Most people mean well.

Not: do we have history? History is not the same as quality.

More or less.

That is the test.

The people who consistently leave you feeling more like yourself: those are your people. Keep them close. Tend that circle with everything you have.

And the people who consistently leave you feeling slightly less: release them with kindness and without guilt.

Your circle is not a reward for the people in it.

It is the environment in which you grow.

Choose it accordingly.

Simone called on New Year's Eve at eleven fifty-eight.

Not to count down. They had stopped performing the midnight countdown ritual in ninth grade when both of them had admitted they found it exhausting.

She called because it was almost a new year and Nova was her person and she wanted to hear her voice at the threshold of it.

"How are you?" Simone asked.

"Really good," Nova said. "Honestly. Really good."

"The gap year?"

"The gap year."

"I'm proud of you," Simone said.

"I know," Nova said.

"You're supposed to say thank you."

"Thank you," Nova said. "I'm proud of me too."

"I know," Simone said.

They laughed at exactly the same time. The specific synchronized laughter of two people who had been finishing each other's thoughts since they were twelve years old.

"Happy New Year Nova," Simone said.

"Happy New Year Simone," Nova said.

They stayed on the phone for another hour after that.

Not because they had anything specific to say.

Because they were each other's people.

And that was enough.

That was everything.

She Arrived — Reflection

◆ Who in your current circle makes you feel more like yourself after time with them? Who makes you feel less?

◆ Is there a relationship you have been maintaining out of history or habit rather than genuine connection? What would it feel like to release it kindly?

◆ Who is your Simone, the person who has been telling you the truth since the beginning? Have you told them what they mean to you?

◆ What is the difference between a friend who celebrates your wins and a friend who calls you forward?

> *My circle is sacred. I choose it with intention. I release what drains without guilt. I tend what grows with everything I have. The right people make me more myself. I deserve those people. And I am that person for them. We build each other up. That is what the right circle does. I have found mine. And I will never take it for granted.*

She Arrived

Your circle is the environment in which you grow. Choose it with the same intention you bring to everything else that matters. Because it matters more than almost anything.

CHAPTER 6

Who Are You Online

I posted something today that I was not sure about.
Not artistically uncertain.
Personally uncertain.
It was about my neurodivergence.
Not as a reference in the line work.
Directly.
In my own words.
In my own voice.
I talked about what it actually feels like
to process the world at this volume.
I posted it.
Within an hour I had heard from fourteen people
who said: this is me.
Fourteen people who felt less alone
because I told the truth.
That is what social media is for.
That is the only thing it is for.
Tell the truth.
Find your people.
Everything else is noise.

Nova had been building her online presence since eighth grade.

Four years of consistent intentional work. What reached people. What reached algorithms. The difference between the two and why the difference mattered.

She had gone viral at fifteen.

She had watched the viral moment do what viral moments did: arrive suddenly, generate extraordinary numbers for a brief period, and then settle into a new baseline that was higher than before but not as high as the peak. The platform moved on. The algorithm found the next thing. Her work remained. The people who had found her through the viral post either stayed, because the work continued to reach them, or drifted away, because they had been drawn to the moment rather than the body of work.

The ones who stayed were her people.

The ones who drifted were not.

That was the lesson of going viral that nobody talked about.

The number was not the point.

The quality of who stayed was.

She had developed what she called her three rules for social media during the gap year.

Not as a content strategy. As a personal philosophy.

Rule One: Post the uncertain work.

She had learned this at fifteen. The uncertain work reached people. The certain work, the polished performed version, reached algorithms. She was interested in people. She posted the uncertain work. Every time.

Rule Two: Tell the truth about who you are.

She had been posting her work online for four years before she posted directly and personally about her neurodivergence. Not as a subtext in the line work. Directly. In her own words. The specific description of what it felt like to be her.

She had been afraid of what would happen.

She knew what had happened to the viral piece when a stranger in the comments had called her neurodivergence forced. She knew what it felt like to have the most honest thing about her treated as an aesthetic choice rather than a fundamental reality.

She posted it anyway.

The response had been quieter than the viral piece. More specific. Fourteen messages in the first hour from people who said: this is me. Not I relate to this. This is me. The specific recognition of someone who had felt alone in something and had just found evidence that they were not.

She had cried reading the fourteenth message.

Not from sadness.

From the specific feeling of having told the truth and had it received by the people who needed it.

That was what the platform was for.

Rule Three: Be unreachable sometimes.

This was the hardest rule.

Nova had started taking Sundays off. Not from work. From the platform. The phone stayed face down. The apps stayed closed. Sunday was for the sketchbook and the walks and the long conversations with her parents and the specific quality of attention that was only available when there was no screen to default to.

What she noticed in the weeks after she started doing this was something she had not anticipated.

The work got better.

Not technically. The specific aliveness of it. The thing that came from having unmediated experiences, walking through the neighborhood and seeing the light on a specific wall at a specific moment and having nowhere to put it except inside herself, where it would process and surface later in the work in ways she could not have predicted.

The platform could not have that experience for her.

Only she could have it.

Only by being there without the mediation of a screen.

The Sunday unreachability was not a restriction.

It was a practice of presence.

Here is the question that will save you more time and energy than anything else I can offer you about social media.

Am I using this platform or is this platform using me?

Answer it honestly.

Not the answer that sounds good. The real answer.

If you are using the platform, consciously choosing what to share, using it to connect with things that genuinely inspire and inform you, aware of how it affects your mood and making active choices accordingly, then it is a tool. Use it.

If the platform is using you, if you are scrolling without intention, comparing without choosing to, measuring your worth in metrics, performing your life for approval, spending hours in the comparison trap and emerging feeling smaller than when you started, then something needs to change.

Not necessarily the platform. Your relationship to it.

Nova made a specific decision during the gap year about what she would and would not share online.

The work: yes. The process: yes. The honest truth about who she was, including her neurodivergence: yes. The moments of genuine joy and genuine uncertainty: yes, selectively, when they were true and universal enough to offer something to the people who would receive them.

Her relationships: no.

Her family's private lives: no.

Her inner circle: no, unless they specifically consented.

Her pain in real time: no. The platform was not a therapist. The comments section was not equipped to hold the weight of real grief or real struggle. She would process privately first. Share the lesson later, when she had enough distance to offer it as something useful rather than as something raw that needed receiving.

She would show up as herself.

She would not give herself away entirely.

The distinction was important.

Being authentic did not mean being boundaryless.

It meant being true, within the specific portion of herself she had decided was available for public consumption, and fiercely private about everything else.

She Arrived — Reflection

◆ What is your current relationship with social media: are you using it or is it using you? Answer honestly.

◆ What is the thing about yourself that you have been indirect about online, letting people infer rather than saying directly? What would it feel like to say it clearly in your own words?

◆ What belongs to you privately? What is the portion of your interior that is not for public consumption regardless of how authentic you are being?

◆ What would one Sunday completely off the platform feel like? What would you do with that time?

> *I use the platform. It does not use me. I post the truth. I protect my interior. Authentic is not boundaryless. I am fully myself online within the portion I have chosen to share. Everything else is mine. Sacred. Private. Protected. And that is exactly right.*

She Arrived

The platform can reach people with your truth. But only you can have the unmediated experiences that make the truth worth sharing. Protect your Sunday. Protect your interior. Post the uncertain work. Tell the truth. Find your people. Everything else is noise.

CHAPTER 7

Self Love Is Not a Destination

I had a hard day today.
Not a bad day.
A hard one.
There is a difference.
Bad days happen to you.
Hard days require something from you.
Today required everything.
I did the practice anyway.
Not because I felt like it.
I absolutely did not feel like it.
Because the practice does not care how I feel about it.
It only cares if I show up.
I showed up.
The practice held.
It always holds.
That is what practice is for.

The hard day arrived on a Tuesday in February without warning.

Not from a specific event. Nothing dramatic had happened, no relationship had ended, no project had failed, no external circumstance had collapsed into crisis. The hard day arrived the way some hard days arrived: out of a clear internal sky, a heaviness that settled in overnight and was present when she woke up before she had any logical reason for it.

She lay in bed for an extra twenty minutes.

This was permitted. She had learned to distinguish between the rest that was genuine and the avoidance that was dressed up as rest. Twenty minutes of lying in the specific quiet of not-yet-starting-the-day while her body and brain calibrated: that was genuine. Lying in bed for two hours scrolling her phone and calling it rest: that was avoidance.

Twenty minutes.

Then she got up.

She went to the mirror first.

Before the coffee. Before the sketchbook. Before anything that might serve as a substitute for the thing that needed to happen.

She stood in front of her reflection.

The girl looking back at her was eighteen years old and tired in the specific way that was not physical tiredness. Not performing okay. Not assembling the face that would be presented to the day.

Just the actual face. The one that showed what was real.

She looked at it for a long time.

"I see you," she said out loud. To herself. To the reflection.

Her voice was slightly flat.

She said it anyway.

"I love you."

The words felt like they were traveling from somewhere far away to reach the surface.

She said them anyway.

"I am more than enough."

She did not believe it in that moment. Not fully. Not with the clean certain feeling it had on the good days.

She said it anyway.

The whole ritual. Every line. Not rushing through it. She gave each line its proper space.

By the end something had shifted.

Not dramatically. Not a transformation from heavy to light. More like the specific physical quality of having said true things out loud in your own voice, the way the body registers truth even when the mind is not entirely ready to receive it.

She was still tired.

She was less alone in it.

That was what the practice did on the hard days.

Not fix it.

Accompany it.

Here is what I need to correct about the way the world talks about self love.

It is sold as a destination.

The implication in every wellness caption, every empowerment book, every conversation about the journey of becoming, is that self love is a state you arrive at. A place you reach after enough work. A feeling you unlock and then have, permanently, available to you from that point forward.

It is not.

Self love is a practice.

A daily, imperfect, sometimes-boring, sometimes-glorious, always-necessary practice.

It is the morning ritual said slowly on the days it feels true and said especially on the days it does not. It is the boundary held when holding it is uncomfortable and the choice to hold it anyway because you have decided that your peace is worth the discomfort. It is the sketchbook carried in your hand, your sketchbook, your specific thing, the external symbol of your internal commitment to yourself, even on the days you do not feel particularly committed.

It is choosing yourself.

Not once.

Not dramatically.

Daily. Consistently. Without requiring the feeling of it to be present before you begin.

Nova had days.

The gap year was not a sustained experience of clarity and growth and peaceful self-knowledge. She was eighteen and human and the world was still loud and the practice was not magic.

She had days when she looked in the mirror and the insecurities were louder than the affirmations. Not the specific insecurities of sixth grade. New ones. The specific insecurities of her specific moment. Was the gap year the right decision or was she hiding from the next step? Was her work developing as fast as it should be?

She had days when she compared herself to other artists her age who were already in college.

She had days when she was lonely.

Not the productive aloneness she had cultivated. The other kind. The ache of wanting to be known by someone in the specific way that friendship and family, wonderful as they were, could not fully provide.

She had those days.

And on all of them she did the practice.

The body practice was the one she had resisted longest.

Not the movement itself. The relationship to the movement.

She had grown up in a culture that talked about the body in the language of improvement. Of working toward something. Of before and after. Of discipline as punishment rather than practice. And she had absorbed that language without knowing she was absorbing it.

The gap year was when she decided to change the relationship.

Not because her body had changed. Because she had.

She started moving every day with one specific intention: to honor the body that had gotten her here.

Not the body she was working toward. Not the body she had in some previous season. This body. The one that had carried eighteen years of experience. The one that had processed the world at high volume and found ways to regulate itself and drawn thousands of pages.

This body.

She moved it in ways that felt like celebration rather than correction.

Some days that was a long walk. Some days it was dancing alone in her studio to music that nobody else was going to hear. Some days it was the specific physical pleasure of stretching, the body asking for length and receiving it.

She looked in the mirror differently.

Not with the assessing quality that catalogued what needed attention. With the specific recognition she had learned to bring to her work: the honest assessment of what was actually there, in its actual form, without the overlay of what it was supposed to be.

"I love the body that got me here," she said.

On the good days and the hard days.

Until she meant it.

Until it stopped being a thing she was trying to convince herself of and started being a thing she simply knew.

The financial practice was the one she had least expected to be a self love practice.

She had understood it intellectually. And then she had her first month where the income she had generated covered all of her expenses with a meaningful amount left over.

She had sat with the bank statement.

Not for the number. For the message.

You did this.

She felt something she could not name for a moment.

And then she named it.

Dignity.

The specific dignity of a woman who provides for herself. Who does not have to wait for someone else's permission or generosity to meet her own needs. Who has built something small and real that belongs entirely to her.

That was self love in its most practical form.

Not the feeling.

The infrastructure.

She Arrived — Reflection

◆ What does your current self love practice look like on the hard days, the days when you do not feel like it? What do you do? What do you skip?

◆ What is your relationship with your own body? Are you moving it as punishment or as celebration? What would honoring the body that got you here actually look like in your daily life?

◆ What would it mean to build the infrastructure of self love, the daily practices, the financial foundation, the protected circle, rather than waiting to feel the feeling first?

◆ When did you last say the morning ritual out loud, slowly, and mean every word?

> *I love myself. I am more than enough. Today is going to be an amazing day. I am intelligent. I am strong. I am powerful. Everything I need is already inside me. I am a goddess. I walk like I have ten thousand ancestors protecting me. I do this practice. Every day. Especially today. The practice holds. It always holds.*

She Arrived

Self love is not a destination. It is the daily practice of choosing yourself. Even on the hard days. Especially on the hard days. The practice holds whether or not you feel it holding. Trust it.

CHAPTER 8

Have Lunch With Your Mother

I asked her who she was before she was mine.
She told me.
All of it.
The girl who played piano.
The woman who built something twice.
The person who said yes when she meant no
and spent years learning to say no and mean it.
She told me all of it.
And I sat across from her
and saw her for the first time.
Not my mother.
A woman.
A whole complete magnificent woman
who existed before I arrived in her life
and will exist long after I have built my own.
I have been looking at her my whole life.
I think today was the first day
I actually saw her.

The restaurant had been open for thirty-one years.

Nova knew this because there was a small framed note near the entrance, handwritten, slightly faded, the kind of thing a family business put up when it had survived long enough to be proud of the survival. Thirty-one years. The same family. The same recipes.

She thought about that while they were being seated.

Thirty-one years of the same thing done well.

She wrote it in the margin of her sketchbook: Thirty-one years of the same thing done well is not repetition. It is mastery. There is a difference.

She looked at what she had written.

She would use that later.

She used everything later.

They ordered. Pasta for Nova. Fish for Reina. They talked about the city for the first twenty minutes. The gallery they had been to that morning. The specific piece, a large textile work by an artist neither of them had known before today, that they had both stopped in front of for longer than they had planned.

"She trusted the material," Nova said. "She didn't try to make it do something it wasn't designed to do. She just let it be what it was and built from there."

"That is a life philosophy," Reina said.

"Everything is a life philosophy if you look at it long enough," Nova said.

Reina smiled. "You get that from me."

"I know," Nova said.

The bread was gone.

The pasta had arrived.

Nova put down her fork.

"Who were you before you were my mom?"

The question landed in the space between them and stayed there for a moment, not uncomfortably, but with the specific gravity of something real being asked by someone who genuinely wanted to know.

Reina set down her fork.

She looked at her daughter.

"How far back?" she said.

"All the way," Nova said.

Reina was quiet for a moment. Not hesitating. Deciding where to start.

"I was a girl who wanted to be seen," she said finally. "Before anything else. Before the music and the relationships and the business and all of it. I was a girl who wanted someone to look at her and see her. The whole her. Not the useful version or the pretty version or the strong version. Just her."

Nova felt the words land.

She recognized what they described.

"Did you find it?" she asked.

"Eventually," Reina said. "In the wrong places first. The way most people do. In relationships that asked me to be less of myself in exchange for the feeling of being chosen."

She told her about the relationships. Not all the details. But the shape of them. The pattern. The specific way she had spent years looking for the seeing in the eyes of people who were not capable of providing it, not because they were malicious but because they had not done their own work.

She told her about the music.

The piano lessons at seven. The church choir at nine. The specific quality of being inside music: the feeling she had never found anywhere else of being held by something larger than herself while simultaneously being most completely herself.

"I wish I had not put it down," she said. "Not because it would have changed the trajectory of everything. But because it was mine. And I let the world convince me that mine was less important than what everyone else needed from me."

Nova thought about the sketchbook in the bag.

She thought about January of sixth grade.

"I almost did the same thing," she said. "With the drawing."

"I know," Reina said. "I watched it happen."

"Were you scared?"

"Every day," Reina said simply. "I was terrified that you were going to learn what I learned: that making yourself smaller was the price of belonging. I was not going to let that happen without a fight."

Nova looked at her mother.

"The conversation," she said. "When you made me say it back three times."

"Yes."

"A friendship that requires you to leave your sketchbook in your bag is not asking for your friendship. It is asking for your disappearance."

"Yes," Reina said softly.

"I have thought about that almost every day since sixth grade," Nova said. "Every time I was about to adjust myself for someone else's comfort."

"I know," Reina said.

"Did someone say something like that to you?" Nova asked. "When you needed it?"

Reina was quiet for a moment.

"No," she said. "That is why I said it to you."

She told her about the hospital.

Nova had known the broad outline of the story since she was old enough to ask questions about where she had come from. She had not known the interior of it.

Reina told her.

The grayish green walls and the windows that showed nothing but sky. The specific loneliness of being the strong one in a room full of people who believed you were fine because you had trained them to.

The first time she had chosen someone else's comfort over her own truth. About how that first yes had established a pattern that had taken years and a marriage and a divorce and an apartment in Rowlett with an air mattress and a lake view to finally break.

Nova listened to all of it.

She did not interrupt. She did not try to fix it or reframe it or rush toward the part where it was okay.

She just listened.

The way her mother had always listened to her.

When Reina finished there was a specific quality of silence between them. Not heavy. Not awkward. The silence of two people who had just exchanged something real and were letting it settle.

Nova reached across the table.

She put her hand over her mother's hand.

"You are so much more than I knew," she said.

Reina looked at her daughter's hand over hers.

"You are just beginning to see me," she said. "The way I see you."

"How long have you been waiting for me to ask?" Nova said.

Reina smiled. The real one.

"Since you were old enough to ask," she said. "I was not going to push it. Some things have to be asked for. You cannot hand them to someone before they are ready to receive them."

"I was ready," Nova said.

"I know," Reina said. "I could see it. The gap year did something to your eyes."

"What do you mean?"

"You look outward differently," Reina said. "Like you are seeing things because you want to see them rather than because you are managing how you appear while looking at them." She paused. "That is what the year of being fully yourself gives you. Eyes that are not busy performing."

Nova sat with that.

"You gave me that," Nova said. "The ability to see like that. You and Nana Rose."

"We started it," Reina said. "You continued it. That is how it works."

They ordered dessert.

They stayed for another hour.

When they left the restaurant Nova reached over and took her mother's hand.

Not the way she had taken it as a child.

The way you took someone's hand when you were walking beside them as an equal. As a fellow traveler. As a woman who had just spent three hours seeing another woman clearly and had decided that the seeing was something she was going to keep doing for the rest of her life.

"Thank you," she said. "For all of it. For the morning ritual and the slow circles and the conversation in sixth grade and the fact that you were always fighting for me to be fully myself even when I did not know that was what you were doing."

Reina squeezed her hand.

"Thank you for asking," she said. "You have no idea what it means to be asked."

They walked back to the hotel through the city evening.

Two women.

Two generations.

The same ten thousand ancestors walking with both of them.

She Arrived — Reflection

◆ What do you know about the woman who raised you before she was yours? What would you ask her if you sat across from her today with nowhere to be and all the time in the world?

◆ What patterns do you carry from watching her that you have never consciously examined? Which ones are gifts? Which ones are yours to release?

◆ When did you last let someone love you all the way, not the managed version, not the strong version, but the whole one?

◆ What would it feel like to take her hand not as a child reaching for safety but as a woman walking beside her as an equal?

> *I come from women who survived. Women who built things twice. Women who put things down that deserved to be picked back up. I carry their strength. I learn from their journeys. I go further. With their blessing. With their wisdom. With their love in my bones and their resilience in my blood. I am the next generation. I go further. That is the gift. That is the inheritance. I receive it fully.*

She Arrived

She was figuring it out the whole time. Just like you. Just like every woman before you. Ask the question. Have the lunch. Let her tell you all of it. You are both ready.

CHAPTER 9

Build Something Yours

I got my first significant commission today.
A brand that makes art supplies.
They want six original pieces
to use in their campaign.
I negotiated the fee.
Not the first number they offered.
I asked for more.
They said yes.
I sat with that for a long time.
Not the money.
The yes.
The specific yes of the world agreeing
that what I make has the value I say it has.
I built this.
Nobody gave it to me.
Nobody helped me design it.
I built it.
And the world said yes.
That is what building something yours feels like.
Remember this feeling.
Build more.

The brand that reached out to Nova had found her through the viral piece.

Not the piece itself. The conversation around it. The specific discussion that had developed in the comments about the line work and the technique and the neurodivergence visible in the patterns. An art director at a company that made high-quality drawing materials had read that conversation and had looked at Nova's full body of work and had sent her a message that was professional and specific and clearly written by someone who had actually spent time understanding what she made before reaching out.

She had read the message three times.

Then she had called her mother.

Not for permission. Not for validation. For the specific practical resource of someone who had built a business from scratch and understood the mechanics of negotiating a contract.

Reina had helped her think through it. Not written it. Helped her think through it. The difference between what they were offering and what the work was worth. The fact that a brand wanting to use her work for a campaign needed her more than she needed them, not because she was not interested, but because authenticity in art supply marketing could not be manufactured and she had the specific authenticity they were paying for.

"Ask for more," Reina said.

"How much more?"

"Double what they offered and settle for one and a half times."

Nova had asked for double.

They had countered with one and a half.

She had accepted.

She sat with the signed contract in her hands and felt the specific solidity of a thing that was entirely real.

Here is what I want you to understand about building something yours.

It does not start with the significant commission.

It starts months or years before the significant commission, in all the unglamorous work of building something from nothing. The first thirty-five dollar print. The raised prices. The Sunday financial check-ins. The daily showing up to make the work even when nobody was watching and the platform was quiet.

Building something yours is not a dramatic event.

It is a practice.

The same way self love is a practice. The same way the morning ritual is a practice.

Nova had been building for six months before the commission arrived.

The commission arrived because of those six months.

Not despite the daily unglamorous work.

Because of it.

She had a failure during the gap year.

She wanted to tell you about it because the gap year narrative can sound from the outside like everything went smoothly.

It did not.

In October she had accepted a commission from an individual buyer, a private person who had seen her work online and wanted a custom piece. The commission had seemed straightforward. The brief was clear. The timeline was reasonable.

And somewhere between agreeing to the brief and delivering the work she had made a decision, a small one, that had taken the piece in a direction the client had not asked for and did not want.

The piece was better.

She knew it was better. But the client had not asked for elevated. They had asked for what they had asked for. And she had delivered something else.

The negotiation that followed was uncomfortable. Not hostile. But uncomfortable in the specific way that situations were uncomfortable when you had made a mistake and needed to own it.

She offered to redo it.

The client accepted.

She redid it, to brief, exactly to brief, her creative instincts held in service of the client's actual need.

They were satisfied.

She wrote in her sketchbook:

> *Lesson learned.*
>
> *There is a difference between commissioned work and personal work.*
>
> *In personal work your instincts serve you.*
>
> *In commissioned work your instincts serve the brief.*
>
> *Know which kind you are making.*
>
> *Before you make it.*
>
> *Not after.*
>
> *This lesson cost me time and discomfort.*
>
> *It was worth the cost.*
>
> *I will not pay it twice.*

She had not paid it twice.

She had refined her client process: added a check-in midway through every commission, a single photograph of the work in progress sent to the client with a specific question. Is this consistent with your vision? A small addition. An enormous prevention.

The failure had improved her practice.

That was what failures did when you were paying attention.

Here is the thing about building something yours that will save you from the specific anxiety that stops most people before they start.

You do not have to know the destination.

You do not have to have a five year plan or a business model or a fully articulated vision of what it becomes. You do not have to be certain it is going to work before you begin.

You only have to begin.

With what you have.

From where you are.

With the specific combination of what you can do and what you love doing and the willingness to do the unglamorous daily work of building before the building is visible to anyone who is not you.

Nova started with a sketchbook.

She built to a viral piece.

She built to the National Showcase.

She built to a brand commission during her gap year.

She will keep building.

Not because the destination is clear. It is not. It shifts and expands every time she reaches what she thought was the edge of it. But because the practice of building is itself the point. The daily showing up. The consistent investment in the work. The specific dignity of a person who has decided that what they make matters and has acted accordingly.

That practice does not stop.

It does not have a completion point.

It is the whole work.

The lifelong work.

And it begins, always, every time, for everyone, with one first step.

Whatever your first step is.

Take it today.

She Arrived — Reflection

◆ What is the thing you want to build that is specifically and completely yours? Not what would be impressive, not what is practical, not what other people expect. What do you actually want to build?

◆ What is the first step? Not the whole plan. The first step. The thirty-five dollar print equivalent. What is yours?

◆ What is a failure you have had that improved your practice once you were honest enough to learn from it?

◆ Are you waiting for the conditions to be perfect before you begin? What would it look like to begin now, with what you have, from where you are?

> *I build something mine. Every day. From where I am. With what I have. I do not wait for the perfect conditions. I do not wait for the complete plan. I begin. I show up. I do the daily unglamorous work of building before the building is visible. I trust the practice. I trust myself. I build.*

She Arrived

You do not have to know the destination. You only have to begin. The thirty-five dollar print is enough to start. Start with that. Build from there. The commission will come when the foundation is ready. Build the foundation.

CHAPTER 10

She Arrived

One year ago I was finishing sophomore year.
I did not know yet what the gap year would be.
I did not know what I would find
in twelve months of intentional becoming.
I knew how to draw.
I knew the morning ritual.
I knew to carry the sketchbook in my hand.
I knew I was enough.
I came in knowing those four things.
Everything else was built on top of them.
The foundation held.
Of course it held.
That is what foundations are for.
I am ready for what comes next.
Not because I have figured everything out.
Because I have figured out
that the figuring out never ends.
And I am at peace with that.
That is what arriving feels like.
Not completion.
Peace.

The last day of the gap year arrived on a Tuesday.

Not a significant Tuesday. No ceremony attached to it. No external marker that distinguished it from any other Tuesday in June. The day she had designated as the end of the formal gap year and the beginning of whatever came next was a day like any other day. Warm. Ordinary. Full of the specific unhurried quality of summer mornings.

She woke up at her usual time.

She went to the mirror.

She said the words.

Slowly. Every one. The way she had been saying them since she was old enough to stand beside her mother at the bathroom mirror and repeat what Reina said. The way she had rushed them in sixth grade when the girl saying them was not quite herself and the way she had said them slowly and meant them again when she had remembered who she was.

She said them now with the specific quality they had acquired over eighteen years of practice. Not the quality of something new being learned. The quality of something deeply known being reaffirmed.

I love myself.

True.

I am more than enough.

True.

Today is going to be an amazing day.

True, not because she knew what the day held but because she had decided it was going to be true.

I am intelligent. I am strong. I am powerful.

True.

Everything I need is already inside me.

True. More true today than it had ever been.

I am a goddess.

True.

I walk like I have ten thousand ancestors protecting me.

True. She felt them.

She looked at the woman in the mirror.

Eighteen years old and complete in the specific way of someone who had given herself the year she needed and had arrived at its end with more than she had come in with.

"There she is," she said softly.

There she was.

She spent the morning in her studio.

Not working toward anything specific. Not building toward a deadline or a portfolio goal. Just drawing, the way she had drawn on the first day of the gap year, with the pure unmediated pleasure of someone who had been doing this since they were nine years old and had never once stopped finding it extraordinary.

The work that came out that morning was quiet.

Not dramatic. Not the viral piece or the National Showcase work. Just drawing. The morning light on the objects on her desk. The specific texture of her favorite pencil against the paper she had bought with her commission money.

She drew for two hours.

She looked at what she had made.

Simple. Precise. True.

The work of someone who had nothing to prove.

She had not understood until this moment how different it felt to make work with nothing to prove. The work made purely because making it was what she did and what she loved.

This was the work she had come to the gap year to find.

This specific quality of making.

She had found it.

Nana Rose called at noon.

Not because she had known it was the last day of the gap year. Nova had not told her the specific date. But Nana Rose had a way of calling at exactly the moments that mattered without being told when those moments were.

"How are you baby girl?" she said.

"Good," Nova said. "Really good."

"Tell me."

Nova told her about the morning. About the drawing. About the specific quality of making work with nothing to prove. About what she had found in twelve months of intentional becoming.

Nana Rose listened.

When Nova finished there was the specific quiet that Nana Rose used when she was about to say something that mattered.

"Do you remember what I told you?" she said. "The morning of your first day of middle school?"

"You were born knowing exactly who you are," Nova said. "The world is going to try to make you forget. Your only job is to remember."

"Yes," Nana Rose said.

"I remembered," Nova said.

"I know," Nana Rose said. "I could hear it in your voice the moment you picked up."

Nova looked at the morning drawing on her desk.

"Nana," she said.

"Yes baby girl."

"I think I arrived."

A pause. The specific pause of someone receiving something important.

"Tell me what it feels like," Nana Rose said.

Nova thought about it.

"It feels like a Tuesday," she said. "Like an ordinary Tuesday morning where everything is fine and the light is good and I made something true in my studio and you called at exactly the right moment." She paused. "It does not feel like I expected it to feel. I expected it to feel dramatic. Like a finish line."

"And?"

"It feels quiet," Nova said. "Specific. Like knowing. Not performing knowing. Just actually knowing. Like looking in the mirror and not having to convince myself of anything. The words are just true. Not things I am working toward. Things I already am."

Nana Rose was quiet for a long moment.

"That is exactly what it feels like," she said. "I arrived at that place once. You will arrive at it many more times. It comes and goes, that quality. Some seasons you have it and some seasons you are building back toward it. But you know now what it feels like. And knowing what it feels like means you will always know when you have drifted from it."

"And know the way back," Nova said.

"And know the way back," Nana Rose confirmed. "Always the same way."

"The morning ritual," Nova said.

"The morning ritual," Nana Rose agreed. "And the sketchbook in the hand."

"And the honest work."

"And the honest work."

"And the circle."

"And the circle."

They were quiet together for a moment. Two women, one eighteen, one in her seventies, in different cities, connected by the specific thread of love that had been built across the whole of Nova's life.

"I love you Nana," Nova said.

"I love you Nova girl," Nana Rose said. "More than you will know until you have your own."

She called her mother that evening.

Reina answered on the second ring.

"Hey baby," she said.

"Hey Mom," Nova said. "I think I arrived."

A specific silence. The kind that held something.

"Tell me," Reina said.

So Nova told her. About the Tuesday morning and the drawing with nothing to prove and the specific quality of saying the words in the mirror and meaning them completely without effort. About Nana Rose's call. About what arriving felt like from the inside.

Reina listened to all of it.

When Nova finished she was quiet for a moment.

"I know that feeling," she said.

"When did you find it?"

"Later than you," Reina said. "But I found it. Not despite everything I went through. Because of it. Every hard season was building toward it." A pause. "That is the truth I wish someone had told me at eighteen. That the hard seasons are not obstacles to arriving. They are the road."

Nova sat with that.

"Nothing we experience is by chance," she said.

"Nothing," Reina said.

"And if we lose ourselves along the way"

"It was all to find ourselves," Reina finished.

Nova looked at the drawing on her desk.

At the stack of sketchbooks on the shelf. Fifteen of them now. The record of ten years of showing up to the page. Of carrying the sketchbook in her hand. Of doing the uncertain work and posting it and letting the people who needed it find it.

Of saying the words in the mirror every morning until they became the truest thing she knew.

"Mom," she said.

"Yeah."

"Tell me your story sometime. All of it. From the very beginning."

A long pause. Warmer than the previous ones.

"I think I am ready to," Reina said. "I have been getting ready for a while."

"I am ready to hear it," Nova said. "All of it."

"I know," Reina said. "I could hear it in your voice the moment you called."

She arrived.
Not at a destination.
At herself.
Which was always the only place worth going.
Tomorrow the next chapter begins.
College applications.
New structures.
New challenges.
New versions of the same essential question:
will you remain yourself
when the world gives you reasons not to?
The answer is yes.

It has always been yes.
It will always be yes.
Because I know the way back now.
The morning ritual.
The sketchbook in the hand.
The honest work.
The circle.
The mirror.
The words.
I know the way back.
I will always know the way back.
Nothing I experience is by chance.
Nothing I lose will be lost forever.
Everything was moving me toward this.
Toward myself.
Toward the woman I was always becoming.
She arrived.
And she is never going away again.
And now, whenever you are ready,
whenever the moment finds you,
you can read her mother's story.
The woman who forgot herself
and found her way back.
The woman who learned,
too late, and then just in time,
that she had always been enough.
She is waiting for you.
Remember Her.

She Arrived — Reflection

◆ What is the thing you want to write on the first page of your next chapter? What word, what sentence, what declaration belongs at the beginning of what comes next?

◆ What does arriving feel like for you? Not the dramatic version. The quiet Tuesday morning version. Have you felt it? When?

◆ What is the way back for you when you drift? The morning ritual, the sketchbook in the hand, the honest work, the circle. What is yours?

◆ Say the whole morning ritual out loud right now. Every word. Slowly. Meaning all of it.

> *I love myself. I am more than enough. Today is going to be an amazing day. I am intelligent. I am strong. I am powerful. Everything I need is already inside me. I am a goddess. I walk like I have ten thousand ancestors protecting me. She arrived. And so will I. Nothing I experience is by chance. I am moving toward myself. Every single day.*

She Arrived

She arrived on a Tuesday. Not at a finish line. At herself. Which was always the only place worth going. You are on the same road. Keep going.

Nova arrived.

She arrived on a Tuesday morning in June with the light coming through her studio window and a drawing on her desk that was quiet and precise and true. She arrived because of the women who held her. She arrived because of the daily practice. Because of the sketchbook in her hand.

And she arrived because of the journey.

The whole journey. Not just the triumphant parts. The sixth grade hallway. The sketchbook in the bag. The months of holding herself still. The heartbreak moved through without shrinking. The gap year and the financial foundation and the commission and the lunch with her mother.

She arrived because she kept going.

And so will you.

This is the book I wish someone had handed me at eighteen. Before the years of learning things the hard way. Before the hospital and the marriage and the divorce and the air mattress and the sixteen hour drive with a toothache and tears on my face and my whole life in the back of a moving truck.

I arrived too.

Later than Nova. But I arrived.

And standing on the other side of all of it, with this series in my hands and my daughter's face in my mind and the morning ritual on my lips every single day without exception, I want you to know:

The hard seasons are not obstacles to arriving.

They are the road.

Nothing we experience is by chance.

And if we lose ourselves along the way, it was all to find ourselves.

Keep going.

She is waiting for you.

With all my love,

Kendra Tamika

ACKNOWLEDGEMENTS

This book would not exist without the people who held me and the people who inspired me.

To my daughter: you are Nova. You have always been Nova. Every word of this series was written for you. For the woman you are becoming. For the daughters you may one day have. For the legacy of women who remember themselves that I want our family to be known for.

To my mother: for Nana Rose. For the wisdom that became the spine of this entire series. For raising a woman who eventually remembered herself.

To every young woman who is standing at eighteen or nineteen or twenty-two in the middle of figuring it out: this book is for you specifically. You are not behind. You are not lost. You are in the middle of becoming. Give yourself the grace.

To the women who came before me and built things twice and kept going when they had every reason not to: I carry you. Every single day. In the morning ritual and in the work and in the way I am raising my daughter to walk into every room like she belongs there.

Because she does.

Because we all do.

Remember her.

She is you.

Also by Kendra Tamika:

Remember Her

The moment a woman stops searching for power and realizes she already is it.

She Always Knew — For the girl ages 6 to 9

She Remembered — For the girl ages 10 to 13

She Rose — For the girl ages 13 to 17

www.ingramcontent.com/pod-product-compliance
Lightning Source LLC
LaVergne TN
LVHW010832120826
845149LV00016B/972